The Immigrants

by Nick Carlo

PublishAmerica
Baltimore

First printing

ISBN: 1-4137-6846-6
PUBLISHED BY PUBLISHAMERICA, LLLP
www.publishamerica.com
Baltimore

Printed in the United States of America

Chapter 1
The Early Years

Surrounded by acres of growing corn, the small town of Drew, Nebraska, faced a crisis. Just one of hundreds of towns in our nation's Corn Belt, Drew's farmers struggled to harvest their crops in time to avoid possible economic disaster.

In 1929, news of the stock market crash sent waves of concern throughout the nation's heartland. Corn growers watched prices plummet drastically, and worried their crops would not yield enough money to save their farms. Once-prosperous families tightened their belts to avoid losing the land that their forefathers fought and died for. Now the Depression threatened to wipe out everything they had worked so hard for. Elderly couples stood by, watching their corn rot on the stalks as farm owners laid-off field hands, finally forcing them into bankruptcy and ruin. Their life savings swept away, victims of a corrupt banking institution.

Families fought within themselves trying to find a solution, but to no avail. Breakups resulted as sons and daughters left home to strike out on their own, hopefully for greener pastures. Husbands and wives divorced, and suicides took a toll on the weak and struggling masses.

Large metropolitan cities throughout Nebraska and all over the country were inundated with job seekers from rural areas begging for food and shelter. With barely enough to feed their own, city fathers had little choice but to offer what little they had to the indigent farmers. Erstwhile farm owners brought what little food they had left, which were mostly vegetables in an effort to help feed the hungry. Shop owners, in turn, provided clothing and blankets to the most destitute.

Louis and Betty Varga, children of Hungarian descendants, met in America after their parents migrated here in 1901. The elder Vargas and Horvaths enslaved in Hungary eked out a living for land owners working for food, clothing and a place to live.

Both families dreamed of coming to America. The oppressive living conditions under the dictatorship of the Hungarian monarchy was totally unacceptable. Marshal law was the rule of the land, and police brutality was rampant.

Selling everything they owned except the clothes on their backs, Julius Varga and Frank Horvath, with their wives, purchased passage with the last of the money they were able to scrape together. They sailed on an antiquated ship for the voyage to the new world. Rough seas, very little food and poor toilet facilities made the trip almost unbearable, but the dream of living in the land of milk and honey banished the dread of the appalling days at sea, and they persevered.

Disembarking at Ellis Island, the two families were isolated. After their medical records were examined and their passports screened and verified, they passed through customs. The New York Port Authority ferry then transported them to Manhattan Island. At an assembly point in the city, they were directed to a Hungarian welcoming and dispatching organization for newly arriving immigrants. Through this agency they could apply for and be granted travel vouchers to anywhere in the country, providing they were financially able to support themselves on arriving at their designated destination. Those unable to do so were given the opportunity to work for the agency until they earned enough money to move on. The jobs were mostly menial labor such as dish washing, garbage collecting and street cleaning. All demeaning work, but for the strong of heart and body, nothing could deter them from reaching their ultimate goal.

Three years of laboring in the kitchens and streets of New York was a hardship, especially for Katrina Varga and Gizella Horvath. Both women bore children, adding to their already burdened lives. The birth of the children in 1902, though untimely, was a welcome blessing. Babies Louis Varga and Betty Horvath furthered the resolve of their parents to a greater degree. By now the couples had become good friends, each sharing their hope of the good life for themselves and their children. A year later they fulfilled their internship and, with their families, moved to their new homestead on the plains of Nebraska.

The work was hard, the hours long, but the Vargas and Horvaths made the best of what they had. Friendly, they easily fit in with their neighbors in the newly founded town of Drew. The townsfolk, many of who were also immigrants from Europe and Asia, banded together to build shops, schools and churches, then pooled their resources and opened the First Savings and Loan Bank of Drew. It was a calculated risk, but the families knew they had to rely on each other if they wanted to succeed.

The first few years demanded sacrifice. Cabins had to be built before the harsh Nebraska winter set in. Water wells were dug and crops were planted. Food supplies and wood for fireplaces and cooking stoves were stored. The community banked on their crops surviving the first winter. The Savings and Loan held the life of Drew in its vaults. Payments on mortgages would come due after the fall harvest. It would be a long, hard winter.

Survival was the key the first spring in the new world. A heavy snow blanketed the Nebraska plains. Frigid air blew down from Canada, threatening the crop of winter wheat many farmers had planted. The first sign of changing weather began to materialize as the snow melted and early blooming wild flowers inched up through the slowly warming earth. Farmers took to the fields, inspecting their crops. Julius and Frank gathered their families around them and thanked God for the blessing of the abundant and rich flowing fields of wheat. Others were not as fortunate, and Drew was saddened when they packed up and moved away. Where they went and if they survived was a question left unanswered. None were heard of again.

A new era began in Drew. After the first harvest in the fall of 1908, the farmers united and decided that planting corn would be the most profitable crop. It would also insure that if a neighbor's crop failed, he could rely on his friends to help him replant and not lose his land. This decision started a trend that spread throughout Nebraska, and corn begin growing over acres and acres of the land. It soon became known as the Cornhusker State.

The next ten years were prosperous ones for the Vargas and Horvaths. They built new homes, added outbuildings to shelter chickens, and raised a barn and silo for their corn. They purchased milk cows and a small herd of cattle.

The children, now 15, were growing up healthy and happy. They helped with the chores and were like brother and sister.

One of the most eventful times in the lives of the two families was the day they became naturalized citizens. It took place on July 4, 1916, Independence Day. How proud they all were, standing there reciting the Pledge of Allegiance to the flag of their adopted country and being congratulated as fellow Americans. It was a dream of a lifetime fulfilled.

Unrest on the European continent troubled Hungarian-Americans, especially the Vargas and Horvaths. The assassination of the Austrian king became a prologue to war. Germany declared war on Austria-Hungary, and Europe exploded into hundreds of bloody battlefields, as Kaiser Wilhelm's troops slaughtered thousands of freedom-loving people. England, France, Russia and finally the United States were drawn into the conflict.

Too old to fight for their country, the couples left their farms and moved to the city to work in factories, supporting the war effort.

World War I, the war to end all wars, came to an end in 1918. The German forces, overwhelmed and beaten, surrendered unconditionally. Triumphant, America's fighting men returned home to the cheers of their fellow countrymen.

Weapons of war were converted to peaceful enterprise, and the country moved back into peacetime prosperity. Back on their farms, Julius and Frank began planning for next spring's planting. An unusually cold and snowy winter was being predicted for Drew and most of Nebraska. The men took all necessary precautions against the weather, then, with their families, they settled in and waited out the winter months.

Chapter 2
Love and a Passing

During their high school years, Betty Horvath and Louis Varga began to notice each other as more than simply friends. At 18, and seniors in the graduating class of 1920, their high school experience brought them closer to the reality of life as man and woman.

Betty was a ravishing young lady. Blessed with classic Gypsy features, she wore her dark, shoulder-length hair flowing around her face. Her dark brown eyes sparkled like diamonds set above high cheekbones. Her full, pink lips, void of lip gloss, featured an angelic smile. When she moved, her body flowed gracefully, like a butterfly in a gentle breeze. She was soft-spoken, and her demeanor was like a love song, gentle and touching.

Louis was a strikingly handsome man. Tall, with a shock of dark, wavy hair, he was his father's son. Sharply defined facial features, swarthy, but finely etched with steel gray eyes and a firm jaw, gave him the rugged look of an outdoorsman.

With their children away at school attending the University of Nebraska, the Vargas and Horvaths found managing their growing workload increasingly tiresome. Growing corn had become a big business. The demand was exceeding the supply, which made it necessary to plant more acreage. The chicken and egg production had doubled, and over the winter their herd of cattle swelled with the birth of several new calves. Julius and Frank, both conservative men, realized that without more help they could not continue to grow and prosper, so they went into Drew to recruit able-bodied farm hands.

Christmas 1922 was a doubly festive occasion. Betty and Louis came home for the holidays to celebrate their parents 30th wedding anniversaries. Both couples were married in the Church of the Holy Innocence, in the town of Majar in Hungary, the Vargas home. The Horvaths came to Majar from their small village several miles away. It was a joyous gala, a rebirth. It was the first time since arriving in America that they could look back and see how they have been blessed. They relived their youth, how they found each other, their struggles and their bitterness, then joy in their new homeland, and they remembered the euphoria of sailing past the Statue of Liberty welcoming them to the shores of America.

Now with their children, a home and a comfortable living, what more could they ask for but continued health and happiness?

The winter of 1923 was a savage killer. Influenza was ravaging Europe and Asia. The sick and dying had reached epic proportions, and the smell of death permeated the air with a vial stench. In America, every precaution was being taken to keep the deadly virus from reaching her shores. The Immigration and Naturalization Authority blockaded U.S. ports, refusing ships entry, and forcing them back into international waters. Those immigrants recently admitted in New York and other ports of entry were ordered interred in camps, quarantined and classified as public health hazards.

On the plains of the heartland, and on farms all over the state, Nebraskans stayed home. Businesses shut down. Classes were canceled in schools, and sporting and social events were postponed. People were warned to avoid large gatherings to minimize contracting and spreading the disease.

Very little was known of this strain of the virus. Overseas they were unable to find a cure soon enough to quell the rapidly growing menace.

At home, the Vargas and Horvaths, with Betty and Louis home from school, prepared for the worst. The houses were scrubbed, clothes washed, and the food and drink supply zealously guarded. The family pets were put in the barn with the other animals. Louis purchased what medicines he thought would help fight off the plague. Now it was wait, hope and pray.

On New Year's Day in 1924, one of the Horvath farm hands returned from Drew after ushering in the new year at a local tavern. Betty watched as he staggered up to her door and knocked. She opened it ever so slightly and asked him what he wanted.

"I'm sick," the man said, "I need help."

"You're drunk," Betty replied, "go to the barn and go to bed."

Gizella scolded her, saying, "Perhaps he is ill. I should go look in on him."

Frank spoke up, "Mama, stay in here. Let him sleep it off. If anything is wrong, our other man will let us know."

Early the next morning, Gizella awoke before anyone else. Bundling up, she left the house to look in on Demetre, their farm hand. What she found was a retching, deliriously sick man, burning up with fever. Instead of turning away from the afflicted man, knowing it could be the flu, she tried to make him comfortable and ease his pain-wracked body.

Winter storms continued to lash the plains with strong winds and blowing snow. Temperatures were well below zero as life outdoors came to a halt. Only fools ventured out of their abodes, and only then for extreme emergencies. It was for this reason Betty Horvath waded through knee-deep snow some 50 yards to the Varga house. Louis opened the door and quickly pulled her into the warm room.

"Mama is ill," she blurted out, "and Papa is frantic. I don't know what to do."

Katrina comforted her. Embracing the child, she said, "I will come and see."

Julius and Louis nodded in agreement, but they both feared a terrible consequence: the flu.

In their senior year at the University of Nebraska, Louis and Betty were dating steadily. They thoughtfully considered marriage after graduation, and were going to tell their parents at the end of the school year. Now, however, the circumstances being what they were, reasonable doubt entered into the picture, and the family's health and welfare came first.

Katrina bent over the prostrate body of her friend Gizella. She touched her forehead as Betty hovered over her shoulder.

Katrina grimaced and said, "She is burning up. Get me cold towels and the medicine. We must work quickly to break her fever."

The two women sat with Gizella for three days, but her condition persisted. "The medicine is not helping," declared Katrina. "I know an old Gypsy potion that might help." Katrina mixed herbs and liquids she had brought with her from the old country. Stirring them, she forced spoonfuls through Gizella's parched lips. Sitting back, she held Gizella's hand and prayed. Speaking to Betty, she said, "If this does not help, only God can." Exhausted, both women fell asleep.

In the interim, Frank was sent to the Vargas house to be with Julius and Louis.

"They said I was just in the way," Frank stated, "so I come over here."

"Mama is sick," he said in Hungarian. "I'm worried."

The three of them set there conversing in Hungarian and broken English. Finally, they also fell asleep.

Gizella awoke, gasping to catch her breath. Betty took her in her arms and kissed her. She tried to talk, but only managed a weak smile as she grasped Betty's hand. Moments later, she died. She suffered throughout her ordeal, even though everything possible was done to help her. Ironically, she passed away on her 43rd birthday, January 15, 1924.

It was a simple funeral. Father Lazlo, the Catholic priest at Our Lady of Hungary Church, officiated at the burial. The family and a few close friends prayed for the repose of Gizella's soul, offering her up to her maker. As the sun set on the frigid Nebraska plains, she was put to rest in the family plot, ending a day of mourning.

The influenza epidemic had passed, but in its wake, thousands suffered and died. It was a devastating plague that would not soon be forgotten.

A late spring slowed the planting process. Frank, still despondent over the loss of his beloved Gizella, lacked the heart to even till the soil. The families got together and decided that Frank would leave his land fallow and help Julius with his crop.

June 1924. Graduation day at the University of Nebraska. Betty and Louis received their diplomas as their proud parents watched the ceremony unfold. They were also honored as the first two children of immigrant families to earn degrees from the university. That evening, family and friends saluted the couple at a small celebration at the Varga home. Louis and Betty added a surprise to the party when they announced their wedding plans. They would be married on July 4, the day their parents became American citizens.

Chapter 3
The Wedding/Heartache/Sons

An uncommon buzzing began to be heard during starry June nights. At first it blended with the nightly sounds of the Nebraska plains. News from farmers south of Drew began trickling in with reports of severe crop damage by locust. They came in hordes, swarming over the earth, chewing up everything in their path and causing total destruction to the young corn sprouts.

Alerted to the locust invasion, Julius, Frank and Louis decided to set fire to their southernmost acreage when the first wave of insects arrived, hoping it would incinerate the pests and save the rest of the crop. Soaking the fields with gasoline, they awaited the onslaught. At first light the advancing column of locust reached the Varga's farm. Torches in hand, the trio set fire to the land. Smoke billowed high into the morning sky as the flames spread, engulfing the moving mass of insects. The burning fields took a toll on the creeping menace. The smell of burning flesh filled the air with a stench as smoke engulfed the rising sun. At first it seemed like the plan was working, but the locust kept coming. Thousands followed, crawling over the dead, sweeping into the unprotected fields. Before it was over the scavenging horde consumed a swath of corn a mile wide and continued northward, eating everything in their path.

Loss of the crop would have been a serious consequence except for the shrewd financial mind of Julius Varga. He had planned for just this sort of emergency. Investing profits earned from the land, he built a small portfolio of stocks and bonds. Wise trading on the stock market had doubled and tripled his initial investment, and despite this disastrous set back, his family's future was secure.

The community of Drew celebrated the Fourth of July, honoring their country's independence, and the wedding of two of their most loved citizens, Betty Horvath and Louis Varga. It was a gala affair. Students from the graduating class of 1925 organized a reception befitting royalty. The Church of Our Lady was filled to overflowing when Katrina, Julius and Frank arrived. The church bells rang out, calling the faithful together to help join their friends in holy matrimony.

The bride was dressed in her mother's colorful wedding gown, a stunning Gypsy ensemble. Her veiled face could not hide her beauty as she walked arm in arm down the white carpeted aisle with her teary-eyed father. Reaching the altar, Louis took her hand in his and they knelt in solemn reverence before the cross of the crucified Christ, and Our Lady's statue. Father Lazlo blessed the couple as they repeated their vows in English and Hungarian. Tears welled up in the eyes of the congregation as the bride and groom exchanged rings, bonding them together till death would part them. Father Lazlo joined hands with the couple and pronounced them husband and wife. The church resounded with cheers as they turned and walked out. Outside, the proud parents celebrated with their children, seeing in them the fruits of their labor and the dreams of old being fulfilled in their flesh and blood.

A letter from the old country set off a chain of events that altered the lives of Frank Horvath and daughter Betty. When Frank and Gizella left Hungary, they said goodbye to Frank's mother and father. It had been very difficult for Frank to leave his parents, since he was an only child and they depended on him for much of their livelihood. He anguished over his decision and became emotionally distraught. His father, realizing his dilemma, made it known that he would not stand in his son's way. He only wished that they to could go to America. Frank loved his parents and told them if they ever needed him he would return from the New World to be at their sides.

The letter contained sad news. Frank's beloved father had passed away suddenly, and his aging mother was grief-stricken and had no one to turn to. Frank, unhappy since Gizella's death, felt duty-bound to go to his mother's side. Betty implored her father not to go, but to send for her grandmother to live out her life here with them. Julius and Katrina offered sympathy and counseling to help Frank make this life-altering decision.

Louis called a friend in Lincoln who knew the ambassador to Hungry. He pleaded with him to arrange an audience to discuss his father-in-law's dilemma. His friend said meeting the ambassador was a problem, but he would take the case before him and explain the circumstances, asking him to look into it.

Days passed by as Frank nervously awaited news from the Hungarian ambassador. Finally, in mid-July, Louis was contacted by his friend. He told Louis that the American ambassador in Budapest had gone over Frank's plight and suggested that his mother's health would not withstand the long journey to America, and it would be inadvisable to subject her to such a trip.

For the past few months Betty had been feeling out of sorts. She decided to visit her doctor thinking her tension and upset stomach were due to worrying over her father's decision to return to Hungary. Katrina had noticed her morning sickness and guessed that she was with child, but did not mention it to her. She wanted Betty to know the joy of childbirth directly from her doctor.

Frank, his mind made up, prepared to leave. Everything he owned he left for Betty and Louis. He said, "I came to this country with nothing, and I will leave the same way."

Betty begged her father not to go."Papa, I'm going to have a baby," Betty announced. "You will be a grandpa, please do not go. If you leave you may never see your grandchild."

Embracing his daughter, Frank wept. Speaking softly, with tears rolling down his cheeks, he said, "I must go home to my mama; she has no one. You have Louis and now a baby. I love you very much, but I made a promise and now I have to keep that promise."

May 1926. Frank Horvath's departure left a void in the hearts of the Vargas. Betty missed her father very much, but now her mind and body turned to the birth of her twin sons.

Frank and Louis Junior were born on May 30, 1926. The boys are identical in all respects except for a birthmark shaped like a small cross on Junior's left hip. Dark black hair crowned their heads, and like all babies, they were cuddly and cute. The parents were extremely happy, and Julius and Katrina were the proudest grandparents in the state of Nebraska.

Chapter 4
The Crash/Heartbreak/
The Hunt

October 1929. It happened, Black Tuesday. The depression struck in a blink of an eye. Julius Varga's stock portfolio was wiped out. The marked had failed, and investors found themselves on the outside looking in, and finding nothing but poverty,

Julius was in jeopardy of losing his farm and land. For the first time in his life in America, he was in a perilous situation. His full-grown corn crop would not be harvested due to a glut on the market, and the prospects of selling off his grain were all but gone.

Survival was the uppermost thought in Julius's mind. There was enough food, except meat, to get them through the winter. Wild game, especially rabbits, were plentiful, and a few deer fed in the fields around the corn belt. Killing wildlife was not a way of life for the Varga family. It was cruel, and endangered the species hunted, but under the circumstances it became a necessity.

Before the snow began to fall, Louis tore down parts of the Horvath house were he, Betty and the children were living, using the remnants to add an additional room on the Varga home. The two families living together would conserve wood, food and water, and more importantly they would be together through the long winter months.

As the depression slowly lifted over the country, the Vargas' survival was costly. They were forced to sell much of their land to save the homestead. Carpetbaggers roamed the countryside, taking advantage of the farmers' dilemma, buying up acres of land from the most impoverished owners for substantially less than it was worth. Many friends of the Vargas had to pull up stakes and return to their homeland.

May 30, 1933. Frank and Louis Junior celebrated their seventh birthday. The twins were active, growing boys. Having completed their first year of school, they exhibited skills far above their grade level, and seemed destined to achieve greater intelligence. Prompted by their doting grandmother, the boys began speaking fluent Hungarian and were fast becoming bilingual. Julius and Louis tended the farm. Betty taught world history to high school students in Drew while Katrina minded the boys. It was becoming a happier time in their lives.

The family finally received news from Hungary. Frank Horvath wrote that his dear mother Maria has passed away. Since his return to his homeland, even though he still grieved the death of his first love, Gizella, he had taken another wife. His yearning for companionship and love consumed him to such a degree that he courted and wed an old classmate.

"I want to come back to America," he wrote. "It will be good to see you, my daughter, and those beautiful grandsons you tell me about, and of course my wonderful friends, the Vargas."

In the spring of 1934, Betty announced she was expecting her third child. Louis was surprised but happy with the news. Julius and Katrina were overjoyed and hoped the baby would be a little girl. The happy event would take place in late September, hopefully on the 25th, Betty's 32nd birthday.

The summer went by rapidly. The corn had been planted and would soon be ready for harvesting. The vegetable garden was growing an abundance of produce, and shortly Julius and Louis would begin their hunt for wild game.

On September 23, the men were out in the fields bringing in the corn. Betty, on maternity leave, was helping Katrina prepare the evening meal. The twins were outside playing and watching their dad and grandpa work. The baby in her womb had been very active the past few days, and Betty was experiencing mild labor pains. She and Katrina were laughing and making fun of her large stomach, when suddenly she felt an overwhelming sense of depression. Betty's face was flushed. She said, "Something is wrong. I don't know what it is, but I feel sad."

Katrina comforted her, replying, "It must be time to have the baby; don't be afraid." The men hurried in from the fields and rushed Betty to the hospital

Betty labored into the early hours of September 25. The doctors were not overly concerned as she began to deliver. When the baby's head crowned, the cord was wrapped around her neck. Cutting the cord, the doctor immediately began CPR on the tiny infant. Moving her to an oxygen tent, he worked feverishly trying to put a breath of life into her tiny lungs. After ten minutes of frenzied activity, the doctor pronounced the child dead.

Only a mother can relate the sadness in her heart over losing a child she has carried to full-term. Such was the feeling Betty Varga felt. Devastated and guilt ridden, she sensed an overriding fear that somehow she had been negligent, causing her baby's death. It would be many months before she would come to realize it was not of her doing, but God's will.

Baby Gizella Varga, named for her deceased grandmother, was buried next to her the following day. Father Lazlo baptized the little girl and administered the last rites of the church, then placed her in the care of the Angels in Limbo.

It was a birthday she would rather forget, but instead was a constant reminder that would live with her the rest of her life. She mourned little Gizella's death with every feeling in her body. Day after day she fought the demon that plagued her. Louis and her boys were of no solace to her, and when she almost lost her faith, blaming God for her unfounded failure, she collapsed in a nervous breakdown.

Cold Canadian air began drifting onto the Nebraska plains. Winter storms would soon be blowing snow and ice, covering the earth in a veil of white.

Open season on deer brought hunters from Drew and the surrounding areas. Louis and Julius prepared for a weekend hunting expedition. Their gear packed, they set out for their favorite campsite some five miles north of their rangeland.

Early the next morning they took up positions near a water hole and waited for first light. They did not have long to wait. Several doe came to drink, followed by a majestic twelve-point elk. He was an elegant beast, a trophy for the lucky hunter that bagged him. He pawed the earth and snorted in defiance of man and beast. Julius was in awe of the huge animal and hesitated just a second before firing his rifle. The elk turned just as the slug ripped into his flank. He dropped to the ground, wounded, but staggered to his feet, bellowing out in anger. Julius raised his gun to fire again, but the elk was on him before he could pull the trigger. The angry animal thrust his massive body at Julius, knocking him down. The elk rolled over him and hooked him with his razor-sharp antlers, ripping a deep gash in his leg. Julius cried out for help as the beast pawed the ground, ready to crush out the life of his antagonist.

Louis, watching the struggle between man and beast, was momentarily paralyzed. Regaining his composure, he realized that Julius was in serious trouble. Raising his rifle, he took careful aim and squeezed off a shot. The animal was charging, head down, when the bullet found its mark. It dropped dead at the feet of the injured and horrified Julius Varga.

Louis did what he could to relieve the pain Julius was suffering. He wrapped the bleeding wound and placed splints on his leg. Using his canvas tent and poles, he fashioned a makeshift stretcher, laid Julius on it, covered him with blankets and pulled him safely back home. The next day he returned to the campsite and brought back the elk.

Chapter 5
U-Boat/Clouds of War/ Twister

The winter months of this fateful year passed ever so slowly for the Varga family. Betty's return to normalcy was a tedious, heartrending, day-by-day battle. Her mind's eye reflected the tragedy she had gone through and kept her out of touch with reality.

Katrina had experienced a similar problem in her youth, though not of losing a child. She lovingly and affectionately drew Betty to her, imposing her will upon her, and eased the pain and suffering from the depressed and frightened young mother. By spring of the New Year, Betty was well on her way to a full recovery.

Julius did not fare as well. His wounded leg became infected, and he lay in his bed, feverish and hallucinating. Doctors tried to set his shattered leg, but the damage was so extensive they could do little, leaving him with a crippling limp.

For the next few years Louis carried the workload around the farm, and Betty returned to teaching. Against his father's wishes, Louis sold off more acreage and invested the money in oil stocks. A calculated risk, but one that would pay handsome dividends. The neighboring state of Oklahoma was awash in oil. Rigs dotted the countryside, and gushers were surging up out of the earth at record numbers.

1939. War machines of the German empire were once again threatening Europe. Adolph Hitler, a self-styled dictator, had illusions of conquering the world. His Nazi ideals favored an Aryan race of men and the extinguishing of the Jewish bloodline. His storm troopers goose-stepped into Poland, routing the Polish army in his first step to rule the world.

Frank Horvath was aware of the impending struggle taking place in Hitler's Germany. Hungary would not be able to withstand the Nazi juggernaught that would spill over the countryside, spreading terror and death, wiping out thousands of his fellow countrymen. He gathered together his meager belongings, and with his wife fled to France and across the English Channel to Great Britain. There he acquired pauper's passage in the hold of the *Lusitania*, sailing for America.

The same day the Vargas heard the shocking news of the sinking of the *Lusitania* by a German U-boat in the Atlantic Ocean, they received a letter from Frank Horvath. Betty anxiously began reading her father's letter but stopped abruptly, dropping the letter. Louis picked it up and read it silently, then broke the news to Katrina and Julius.

The sinking of the *Lusitania* marked the entry of the United States into the war with Germany. Hitler's armies were sweeping across Europe. England was under siege by the Lufwaffa, dropping tons of bombs. London burned day and night. The Russian border was pierced, and thousands of German troops swarmed over the countryside, headed for Moscow.

The Varga twins excelled in the classroom and in extracurricular activities, carrying away the honors of Drew's graduating class of 1939. Eager to learn, they were voracious readers, reading every book they got their hands on. They were also excellent athletes, playing baseball, football and basketball, and starring in each sport. On the farm they helped their father and grandfather with the many chores that had to be done. Every day they grew in mind and body, becoming young gentlemen.

The oil stock investments Louis made were making a huge difference in the family's financial outlook. They turned a new page in their book of dreams. Two new ranch-style homes now replaced the old homes that served them for many years. New automobiles, one each for Louis and Betty, replaced their antiquated vehicles. A new barn for more farming equipment, and a towering silo for the harvested corn, were also added to the property. Additional heads of cattle roamed the pastureland, and more dairy cows increased milk production. All the amenities needed for the homes were installed and life became less of a struggle. Julius and Katrina, happy with their son's success, nevertheless retained many of the old ways and customs they brought from the old country.

In December1941, the Japanese struck suddenly and with a vengeance at the American naval base at Pearl Harbor, on the Island of Oahu in the Hawaiian Islands. So secret and well planned was the attack that the United States was caught unaware. The attack on Sunday morning, December 7, was devastating. Thousands of our armed forces were killed and injured while much of the Pacific fleet, mostly battleships, were destroyed. It was a dark day in the history of the United States, but even after the decisive victory, Admiral Yamamoto of the Japanese Imperial Navy issued a warning: "I am afraid we have awakened a sleeping giant."

Christmas 1942. Julius and Katrina celebrated their 50th wedding anniversary. What a joyous holiday it was. The family attended midnight Mass on Christmas Eve, and after Mass, Father Lazlo asked the parishioners to stay and help one of Drew's most respected couples celebrate a once-in-a-lifetime event. A round of applause welcomed the Vargas as they knelt at the altar railing. The old Hungarian priest repeated the marriage ceremony, and Katrina and Julius renewed their sacred vows before God and man.

Louis, Betty and the twins hugged and kissed their parents and grandparents as tears of joy trickled down their faces. The congregation fondly expressed wishes for their happiness as the old bride and groom jubilantly left the church. At home, Katrina and Julius sank into their favorite chairs. Sipping a glass of wine, they spoke in their native tongue, reminiscing about their wedding day 50 years before and how happy and in love they were, then and now. Finally, in the glow of the fireplace, smiles were seen etched on their faces as they drifted into a serene sleep.

1943. The war in Europe raged on. Germany, joined by Italy in the fight against the allies, was being pushed back on all fronts. The Russians, in the bitter cold, were rallying and turning the tide against Hitler's army while the U.S. and Great Britain were storming into the Rhineland, heading for Berlin

On May 30, seventeen-year-old Frank and Louis Junior celebrated birthdays and graduated from Drew Senior High School as honor students. Both boys would enroll in the fall at the University of Nebraska, following in their parents' footsteps.

The twins were rascals, using their singular identity to confuse and amuse their peers, teachers, parents and grandparents alike. Extremely patriotic, they were active in civilian service for the armed forces, selling war bonds, working part time in factories, organizing and taking part in USO gatherings, and doing everything they could toward the war effort.

A week later, as the elder Vargas sat on their front porch, a slight wind chilled the air. It had been a warm day, with spotty rain showers. Ominous-looking clouds billowed across the sky, a forewarning of threatening weather. Katrina went into the house for a sweater, and when she returned, rain was pouring down.

She spoke to Julius, "I hope the children are on their way home. This looks like a bad storm." Julius got up out of his chair, looked toward the south, and saw a swirling black cloud dip close to the ground. Before he could utter a word, a funnel cloud formed and touched down a hundred yards from the house. It seemed to hover there, not moving, gathering strength and getting bigger until it was so large it blocked out everything in view.

"We must get to the cellar," Julius shouted over the noise of the tornado. As they moved toward shelter, the storm struck in all its fury.

Louis, Betty and the twins had just concluded a business meeting. The boys wanted permission to enlist in the Army, and they had been speaking with an Army recruiter. On their way home, the storm intensified, and as they neared the farm they began to see signs of severe damage. Trees were down. Electric wires whipped back and forth, spitting fire from their broken ends, and debris filled the dark sky.

Reaching the house, they rushed in, looking for Katrina and Julius. The twins sprinted to the open cellar door, peered in and called to their grandparents.

Katrina answered, "Down here, boys. Grandpa is hurt."

The next day dawned calm and bright. Dr. Janos was treating Julius for his injuries, while Louis was outside surveying the damage the tornado had left behind. The barn and silo were damaged but reparable. All the stock were safe, but the house took the brunt of the storm. Most of the roof was torn loose, windows were shattered, and the porch Julius and Katrina had been sitting on was ripped away from its foundation.

After finishing his examination, Dr. Janos spoke with the family. He told them, "Julius was struck in the head, which resulted in a severe brain concussion. He also re-broke his injured leg, probably from falling down the cellar steps.

"He is in serious condition and should be hospitalized, but he refuses to go." The doctor continued, "His leg needs to be re-set. He may become nauseous, dizzy and disoriented, and all of this could lead to a fatal stroke."

Katrina spoke to Julius, then turned to the doctor and said, "He will go to the hospital."

Betty managed the household while Katrina stayed at the hospital, nursing her husband back to health. Louis and the twins went about cleaning up the destruction left by the twister and making necessary repairs.

Chapter 6
Army/The Bomb/Drought

A special arrangement with the Department of the Army allowed the Varga twins to enlist at age seventeen, with the permission of their parents, and with the stipulation that they not be sent overseas until their eighteenth birthday. They would begin their freshman year of college at the University of Texas in Dallas, in lieu of the University of Nebraska, with an advanced workload recommended by the faculty of Drew High School, and with special training in the Army ROTC.

1944. The war with Germany is over. The Nazi conquest of Europe had failed. Berlin had fallen, and the once powerful German army had surrendered. The war in the Pacific raged on as American forces began retaking island after island, and would soon strike the Japanese on their own soil.

Frank and Louis Junior finished their first year with flying colors. They achieved second lieutenant status in the ROTC and were assigned duty at Hickem Field, on the north shore of the island of Oahu in Hawaii. There they continued to study and learn the finer points of military strategy.

Back home in Drew, Betty took a sabbatical from her teaching position in order to help Katrina run the household. Julius was almost totally dependent on Katrina's care, leaving her with little time for anything else. Louis ran the farm from his office. With new farm machinery and hired hands, he left the fieldwork to his employees. He had repurchased much of the land his father once owned and was operating at peak level. Raising corn was once again profitable.

1945. The United States military was at Japan's doorstep. Wartime commanders planned the final stages to end World War II. The invasion of the home Island of Japan would take a fearful toll of American lives, even if air strikes and naval bombardments pounded them day and night. An alternative method had to be found. Scientists were working on a new weapon, one that would unleash an energy so powerful it could destroy the world if it fell into the hands of the wrong country.

After weeks of agonizing over the use of the bomb, President Harry Truman gave the order. The first use of atomic energy in the form of a bomb was a crushing and devastating blow to the city of Hiroshima. One bomb dropped from a B-52 bomber, the *Enola Gay*, which flattened the city and killed thousands of its inhabitants. A second attack, this time on Nagasaki, ended the conflict. In June, the Japanese government signed terms of unconditional surrender in Tokyo Bay, aboard the *U.S.S. Missouri*, and peace prevailed once more

Postwar America boomed. Factories re-tooled. Automakers begin manufacturing cars by the thousands. Soldiers returning to civilian life found abundant jobs, married and had children. The housing industry flourished. Universities made way for veterans enrolling on the G.I. Bill with government money to get an education. Peace and prosperity was the password as Americans went about living the good life.

The Honorable Harry Stanton, member of the House of Representatives from the state of Nebraska, placed the names of several candidates for review to enter the U. S. Military Academy at West Point, on the Hudson River in upstate New York. Two of these young men, Frank and Louis Varga, exceptional students and ROTC trainees, would be accepted into the first postwar class in September 1945.

Home on leave, the twins spent much of their time visiting friends and reestablishing relationships. By now, the nineteen-year-olds had grown into manhood. Both six feet tall, stocky, and with strong upper bodies, they shared their parents' identities and their grandparents' desires.

As summer wore on, hot winds blew over the plains. A stifling heat wave took its toll on man and beast. Crops began to wither from the searing sun, and farmers prayed for rain. Streams dried up and wells were pumping less water. Weather forecasters were predicting extreme drought conditions and warning the public to conserve water. Thunder rolled over the countryside, and lightning flashed out of empty clouds, but not a drop of rain fell. Topsoil blew into the air from gusting winds, forming tornado-like funnel clouds.

In late August the fields and brush were tinder-dry, and the threat of fire from lightning strikes was becoming a reality. Louis, the twins and the farmhands began harvesting the corn, hoping to cut it down and avoid the possibility of lightning starting a fire. They labored all day and into the night. Ironically, a malfunction in the harvester caused it to overheat and catch fire, igniting the field. They fought the blaze frantically, but conditions were so bad they had to give up to save themselves. Retreating to the farmhouse, they hosed down the house in an effort to keep it from burning. A few days later, Louis surveyed the damage. The barn and silo were scorched. One of the cars was badly burnt, but the house escaped with just smoke damage. Looking out over the devastation, all you could see were blackened fields and ashes. Fortunately no one was hurt, and life went on.

Julius Varga lay on his hospital bed near death. The trauma due to the concussion had increased the swelling in his brain, and he lapsed into a coma. Doctors advised Katrina that if he didn't have surgery to relieve the pressure on his brain he would die, and even if the operation was a success, the chances of a full recovery were doubtful. He would be alive, but in a vegetated state. The family gathered around Katrina, consoling her and promised to support her in any decision she made. The love of her husband over the past 53 years was so strong that she could not bear to live without him. She would not be deprived of his presence, even though his mind may cease to function.

She said, "He must have the operation, and we will pray that Almighty God spare him and restore him to us in mind and body."

As they walked through the gates of the bastion of higher learning, the academy at West Point, the twins stood in awe, marveling over the structure and the mystique surrounding it. They recalled names of men like MacArthur, Patton, Eisenhower and Bradley, knowing they had roamed the hallowed halls of this great institution. They were spellbound and proud to be a part of America's officer corps. As plebes, Frank and Junior were subject to the whims of the upperclassmen. They were the lowest of the lowly, treated like buffoons, but strictly within the rules of military justice. Senior cadets took pleasure in confronting them with types of questions relative to their daily routines, and taunted them for improper answers. It would be an interesting four years for the Varga twins. The academy would see to that.

Classes came easy for the boys, though their antics sometimes got them in trouble. They maintained a 4.0 grade point average, and midway through their first year were astounding their instructors with their work ethic. They also confounded their instructors who were having difficulty recognizing one from the other. They played harmless but annoying pranks on their classmates and teachers that caused disruptions that would not be tolerated. They were soon separated into different classes and the problem was solved, so they thought.

Physical conditioning, as well as academics, were stressed at West Point. Strong minds and bodies were essential for aspiring Army officers. The twins exceeded the records in many of the physical challenges set before them, including earning letters in football, basketball and baseball. After three years they were the top two in their class academically, and were honored as "All Americans" in three sports.

The Varga family prepared for a birthday celebration for their homeward-bound West Point cadets. Though they would not arrive until the first of June, arrangements were in full swing for the happy occasion. It would be a bittersweet homecoming, and the last time they would see their grandfather alive.

After surgery, Julius remained in a coma. The doctors had relieved the pressure on his brain, and only time would tell if the surgery was successful. After weeks in the hospital and no sign of improvement, Katrina took Julius home. Perhaps she said, "In his own bed he will come back to me."

Her heart aching, Katrina spent hours talking to Julius, hoping he would hear her and answer her plea to wake up. Finally, one night as she slept fitfully, she was awakened by muffled sounds emanating from Julius's room. She quickly got up and hurried to his bedroom. When she arrived, Julius was setting up gesturing and babbling wildly in Hungarian. Louis joined Katrina and tried to calm him down, but he went on for several minutes. Finally sinking back into his bed, exhausted, he spoke rationally to both of them, vowing his love, and hugged and kissed his beloved Katrina. Then he lapsed back into a coma.

A rebellion in the Asian country of Korea was about to split it in into warring factions. Communist-controlled North Korea, aided by the U.S.S.R., had designs on taking over the free Republic of South Korea. The United States warned the North Korean government and the Soviet Union that it would not stand for the menacing Communist interference, and if necessary would come to the aid of South Korea.

Happy birthday greetings displayed on large signs welcomed Junior and Frank as they deplaned at the airport in Lincoln. Betty rushed to greet her sons. Gushing with enthusiasm and pride, she gathered them into her arms, hugging and kissing them, and smothered them with motherly love. Louis and Katrina welcomed the boys with hugs and handshakes, then they departed the airport.

On the way home, the boys asked where their grandfather was. They knew he was ill, but had never been told how serious his condition was, so not to worry them while they were concentrating on their studies.

Katrina said, "Grandpa is very ill and couldn't come to meet you." Louis explained the whole situation, and the rest of the trip was in a quiet and somber tone.

July 4, Independence Day, was a beautiful summer day. Betty and Katrina packed a picnic lunch while Louis and the boys made a bed for

Julius in the station wagon. They drove to their favorite campgrounds, a secluded spot near a small lake just minutes from home. Here they spent the day reminiscing about all the good times spent together. Louis, Betty and the twins splashed around in the warm lake water, then basked in the late afternoon sun. As evening approached, they built a campfire, toasted marshmallows and talked until the sun sank and darkness set in. Junior and Frank had visited Drew earlier in the day and purchased fireworks. Armed to the teeth, they began to fill the sky with an array of colors. Sunbursts and multicolored comets streaked skyward, lighting up the dark night. Bombs exploding shattered the stillness while whistling, hissing rockets spewed the colors of the rainbow into the vast expanse of the black sky.

He lived his dream, the Hungarian immigrant, and died in his dream. As the last rocket sped skyward, it carried the soul of Julius Varga to his heavenly home. Forty-six years passed since the humble man stepped foot on U.S. soil after leaving his homeland. His was a success story carved out of the good earth with sweat and toil, sacrifice and dedication. He endured where others failed, and became a model citizen of the country he adopted as his own

Father Lazlo prayed the Mass of Christian Burial, and Julius was laid to rest in the family plot next to his stillborn granddaughter and his lifelong friend, Gizella Horvath.

The family was saddened by his death but carried on. Louis continued raising corn, but only a few acres. The rest of the land he sold, and he invested the money in new postwar enterprises that were solid investments. Betty continued teaching school, and Katrina, still in good health at 76, maintained the household.

In mid-August, Junior and Frank returned to West Point. Their early arrival was for football practice. This was to be their last extracurricular activity during their senior year. They wanted to maintain their 4.0 grade point average and decided to forgo everything else and concentrate on their classes.

After seven weeks the cadets were unbeaten, but looming on the schedule were top ten teams like Georgia Tech, Michigan, undefeated Notre Dame, and their arch rival, the U.S. Naval Academy. No game was as important as the Navy game. The honor of the two academies was at stake. A victory would assure bragging rights for a year, and nothing else mattered. They had to beat the Navy.

Tech and Michigan felt the sting of the Army juggernaut. A week later they played to a 0-0 tie with the "Fightin' Irish." It was a classic battle, leaving Notre Dame and the Army tied for the number one spot in the national polls.

In Memorial Stadium in Philadelphia, Pennsylvania, December 1948, it was showdown Saturday for the rivalry. For the Black Knights of the Hudson it would mean a chance at a national championship. Navy, coming in with a 9-1 record, could doom the cadets' hopes with an upset victory.

Junior and Frank were expected to play a big part in the game and get revenge against the midshipmen for last year's beating. An hour before game time, the Naval Academy middies marched into the stadium, followed by the corps of cadets. Aligned on the field, side by side, they greeted their commander in chief, the President of the United States, and stood at attention during the playing of our national anthem. Then, in memory of the men and women who lost their lives in the fight for freedom, taps was sounded. A lone bugler blew the solemn notes to the silent crowd.

Early in the first quarter, Louis scored a touchdown on a 40-yard sweep around the Navy left side, going in untouched. Navy retaliated with a long pass, as their lone receiver broke free of double coverage and romped into the end zone, tying the score. The two teams battled for three quarters, neither surrendering another score. Frank and Louis alternated at the halfback position; keeping fresh legs in the game gave the Army team a slight advantage on the ground. Louis was faster and more aggressive than Frank, and was gaining chunks of yardage plunging through the Navy defense. Midway through the fourth quarter, Louis broke loose for a long run, but was tackled short of the goal line. The deep safety grabbed his face mask, pulling him down with a vicious twisting tackle. Louis reacted out of character by throwing a punch and wrestled down his opponent. The officials broke up the ensuing fight and penalized both teams fifteen yards for unsportsmanlike conduct, and Junior was warned. The next time he would be ejected from the game.

Disappointed and humiliated over losing his cool, Junior sat on the bench and watched his teammates fumble the ball and lose possession. The turnover eventually cost the Army a touchdown and a 14 to 7 Navy lead.

The Navy mascot, Billy Goat, added his voice along with the cheering midshipmen as they sensed a stunning upset. Now, as the game clock ticked away, the Army needed to launch a comeback. Louis jumped off the bench as he heard his name called, and was sent running onto the field. Back in the game after a tongue-lashing by his coach, Louis ran wild. He ran in and out and around the Navy defense, scoring two touchdowns, beating the Middies with just seconds to play, 21 to 14. As the game ended, a cannon shot echoed throughout the stadium. The Army mule paraded up and down the sideline, braying noisily. Surrounded by their teammates and hundreds of their peers who had made their way onto the playing field, the jubilant cadets silenced the crowd. With the midshipmen, everyone stood at attention and saluted the commander-in-chief as he left the stadium.

In the locker room, pandemonium reigned. Champagne flowed freely, possibly prematurely. Sports writers all over the country were calling in their votes that would determine who would be that year's national champion. The Army's head coach asked for silence. He congratulated his team on its successful season, and especially on the spirit and toughness they showed while beating the Navy in the final seconds of the game. Frank and Louis were claimed most valuable players by their teammates and were showered with champagne. A few minutes later the phone rang in the locker room. By a unanimous vote the Cadets were crowned national champions, and the celebration started all over.

Chapter 7
The Girls

During their junior year Louis and Frank had opportunities to meet and enjoy the company of girls from nearby colleges. Dances at West Point, outings and co-educational class functions brought the young people together. Both of the boys found favor with special girls and began dating on a regular basis.

Violet Spencer and Grace Hunter sat in their college snack bar sipping colas and talking about their boyfriends. Seniors, both girls were discussing their lives with Frank and Louis after graduation. With the fighting in Korea increasing, the United States was sending troops to aid the South Koreans battling the Communist North. It was almost certain that the twins would be sent into the conflict.

June 1949. The police action, as it was referred to, since no declaration of war was formally declared by the United States, raged on throughout the Korean peninsula.

At West Point it was graduation day. The senior class, somewhat uncertain about their future, gathered in the great hall with mixed feelings. Special honors were awarded for various achievements to outstanding cadets. Among those mentioned were Louis and Frank Varga for their four-year 4.0 grade point average. A hushed silence came over the class as each cadet came forward and received his commission as a second lieutenant in the United States Army. Louis, Betty and Katrina stood up and applauded with gusto as the twins were awarded their commissions. They had never been more proud of the boys as they were on that day, but their exuberance was tempered by the feelings of anticipation as the reality of war in Korea hung over them like a dark and ominous cloud.

After the graduation ceremony the boys picked up their dates and joined their parents and grandmother for a celebration party. They introduced Violet and Grace for the first time. They had written often about the girls, but this was the first opportunity to meet them in person.

After their graduation, Violet and Grace were invited to the Varga farm to spend time with the twins. The family came to know and love the girls. They found them gracious and delightful spirits who injected fresh life into everyone around them.

Violet Spencer was a lovely girl. Her fair complexion paled against her dark tresses that curled down to her waist. Her softly colored blue eyes peeked out from under finely detailed brows. Her dimpled cheeks opened and closed each time she moved her velvety lips. She was in essence an all-American girl: smart, good-looking and the image of the "girl next door." She had her heart set on becoming Louis Varga's lover and bride.

Grace Hunter had none of the advantages growing up as did Violet. She came from a poor family of three brothers and three sisters. Family problems plagued the Hunters. The three eldest, all boys, were in and out of trouble with the law. Grace, the oldest daughter, tried to hold the family together, but when her parents separated she gave up and left home. At only 15, she moved to New York and found work as a waitress. She worked hard, saving every penny she could, determined to continue her education. At 18 she enrolled at Wadsworth College and worked her way through four hard years waiting tables in the college dining room and snack shop. She was not endowed with the beauty that God willed Violet, but in her own right was an attractive girl. Tall and full figured, with coal-black hair and dark brown eyes, her face wore a perpetual smile, hiding the signs of the struggle she had already faced in her young life.

The short two-week leave for the twins was almost over. The afternoon mail contained their shipping orders. That evening the family sat anxiously as the boys opened their mail. Junior was the first to speak.

Reading aloud, he said, "I am to report to Fort Bliss, in Dallas. There I will be airlifted, via Military Air Transport Service to Osaka, Japan, where I will join up with elements of the Eighth Army headquartered there, to await further instructions."

Louis continued, "It looks like a jumping-off spot for Korea. What about you, Frank?"

Frank scanned his orders and said, "I'm with you, brother."

Later that evening Louis and Frank broke the news to their parents that they had proposed to the girls and they consented to be their wives.

Louis said, "We asked Father Lazlo to marry us, but he persuaded us not to rush into anything, but to talk it over with you. We agreed and realized we should have consulted you first."

"Boys," Betty replied, "we appreciate your position, and we would not stand in your way. However, fate has a way of intervening in our lives, and with the situation the way it stands, I believe it would be best for all concerned to wait until you come home."

Violet spoke up, "Grace and I have talked it over. She has no particular place to call home, and my parents are vacationing in Europe. We would appreciate it very much if we could stay here until the boys return. We can find jobs in Drew and be together. We love your sons and want to be with them for life."

A few days later, Louis, Frank, Violet and Grace celebrated their formal engagement at a party with family and friends. Each of the girls wore beautiful diamond rings on their fingers, symbolizing the love of their husbands-to-be.

Katrina was never left out of the discussion concerning the marriage of her grandsons. She had listened to all the family members and the girls, but felt it was their decision to make, and kept her feelings to herself until the boys came to her and asked for her blessing. She felt a sense of respect and love that they chose to speak to her about such an important decision, and happily granted them her blessing.

Chapter 8
Training/Politics/Reality

The plane slowly lifted off the runway and pointed its nose into the cloudless sky. The Vargas and their new family watched tearfully and waved goodbye to their loved ones. Their prayers, drowned out by the roar of jet engines, rode with the young soldiers on their journey to whatever the Almighty had in store for them. The next few months or years would challenge the courage of every member of this loving family to hold fast to their love for each other, and never give up hope that their fighting men would return safely

July 1949. Osaka, Japan. Helicopters circled above as the MATS (Military Air Transport Service) flight carrying the Varga twins touched down, ending a long, weary flight from the United States. This Air Force base was a collection and staging area for sorties into firefight camps in South Korea. Fresh troops were shuttled in and out continuously to reinforce the embattled Korean and U.S. troops fighting the North Koreans and hordes of Chinese regulars who had joined sides to overthrow the seat of power in Seoul, the capital of South Korea. Elements of the U.S. Eighth Army were engaging the enemy at Pusan, a critical seaport town in the south. Frank and Junior were hastily billeted into officers' quarters and told to be prepared and stand by for orders. Two helicopter gunships returning from Pusan brought in wounded and dead from the battle site. Minutes later they were refueled, rearmed and boarded with fresh troops.

Lieutenant Louis Varga Junior commanded the first Huey, with a master sergeant and a landing crew of eight. Following in the second copter was Lieutenant Frank Varga and his crew. Separated for the first time in their lives, the twins felt vulnerable. This wasn't West Point or a football game. This was stark, naked reality. The copters lifted off the tarmac as a shrill voice pierced the air over the noise of the whirlybird's blades.

"Now hear this: This a training maneuver. You new lieutenants listen to your sergeants and follow their lead. Your crews are veterans of firefights and know what to do."

Junior and Frank were stunned and relieved. They had no idea of what to do had this been the real thing. Back on the ground, they were informed that for the next two months they would continue to simulate preparation for firefights until they were ready to meet the enemy. The two boys stood there speechless, shaking and sweating.

"My God," Frank said, "what just happened to us, Louis? We just got a look at our future, and it scared the hell out of me. I almost wet my pants!"

Louis swore and said, "We got two months to shape up. Let's do our job and get the hell out of here!"

Back at home, news of the war was not good. Letters from the twins kept the family assured they were all right and were awaiting their first junket into battle-scarred South Korea. Betty, Katrina and the girls busied themselves planning and shopping for the wedding, never thinking the boys would not return. They wrote every day, keeping them informed of life at home and filling their hearts with endless words of love and support.

Louis missed his sons. He missed the male companionship he had shared with them all the years of their young lives. Now, with less farming and little else to do, he had a lot of time on his hands. The summer crop had been harvested and sold. The stock market was stable, and his investments were paying handsome dividends. The hunting season was open, but it was not the same without the twins at his side. He still grieved over his father's death, and it preyed on his mind. When the mailman came he feared he would bring bad news about his sons, but would be happy to hear they were okay.

At 47, Louis needed a new career, a new beginning. Well known in Drew and throughout the state of Nebraska, Louis considered politics and running for office. He was a charismatic man, well spoken, intelligent and with solid connections in local government. His ethnic background would be a plus on the local level, since Drew was an American/Hungarian community. It appeared to be a logical place to begin. He would get feedback from his friends and neighbors, and undertake a quest to ascertain the needs of the entire population of Drew. He would enlist the help of Father Lazlo, Doctor Jonas and his friend of the Hungarian Ambassador who could help him form a committee for his nomination and election as mayor of Drew. Louis unveiled his plan to Betty and Katrina, seeking their opinions and ideas to help promote his candidacy. They pledged their assistance, primarily to swing the women's vote into his camp. Violet and Grace, in the short time they had lived with the Vargas, had made many friends of the young people of Drew and would campaign to bring in the young adult vote.

Elections in Drew were no big deal in the past, but this November was going to be an exception. Since throwing his hat into the political ring and announcing he would run for mayor as an Independent candidate, the city had come alive. The incumbent mayor had not demonstrated equal rights among his constituents, particularly immigrant families. He would find his seat challenged.

Day one for the young lieutenants started at five am on October 1. A hurried breakfast and a briefing on the day's activities was laid out by Colonel Stone, commander of the Eighth Army Mobile Strike Force.

"An ROK platoon of elite forces has encircled one of our patrols. There are eight men pinned down ten miles north of Pusan. It's your job to get in there, relieve these men and get them back here. Once you have accomplished that, dig in and call for an air strike. Make sure your coordinates are correct so the flyboys don't drop their load in your laps. Any questions? Good luck."

A light drizzle fell out of ominous-looking clouds as the men climbed into the helicopters. Louis gave a thumbs-up sign to Frank as he closed the hatch and disappeared into the Huey. The whine of rotor blades broke the morning silence as the birds lifted off and began their journey into the hostile jungle of the Korean countryside.

The pilot's voice boomed over the intercom, "The smoking lamp is lit. You got 20 minutes." Then there was silence, except for an occasional whispered prayer.

The helicopters touched down amid the clatter of machine gun and small arms fire. Smoke grenades clouded the air covering the men as they scrambled from the safety of the gun ship. They hit the ground running. The high brush, wet with morning dew, helped to conceal them as they slowly advanced to a wooded area bordering the river. A smattering of gunfire was the only noise as the men made their way to a pre-set position. The master sergeant mustered out a quick roll call and reported to Lieutenant Louis Varga that all were accounted for. Studying his map, Louis determined a safe crossing point in the river was ten clicks downstream. He ordered a point man to advance, span the river and dig in.

They were behind enemy lines, part of a pincer movement to sweep inland a quarter mile then swing north to join up with Lieutenant Frank Varga's unit moving in from the south. If successful, it would cut off the enemy, blocking there return to their main force.

The firefight proved deadly. Back in Japan the crews were being debriefed. Louis described the battle. "Three dead, three wounded, including my brother. We linked up without a problem and would have had the element of surprise except for a three-man enemy patrol that surprised us. We took them out, but gave away our positions and all hell broke loose." Louis took a big drink of coffee, then continued. "They were well dug in, surrounding our lost patrol, so we had to be extra careful. We were pinned down by machine-gun fire and couldn't advance. I sent two men with grenades. One made it and blew up the machine gun nest. The other man was killed.

Colonel Stone stopped Louis. "Take a break, soldier."

Louis resumed his story. "Lieutenant Frank Varga and I discussed the situation. We checked with our master sergeants and decided to get in close and fast. We made a full frontal attack, charging their line of defense, wiping them out in hand-to-hand combat. At one point I felt a sharp pain in my left shoulder; I thought I was hit."

"I don't see a wound, Lieutenant," remarked Colonel stone.

"No, sir," Louis responded. "When the skirmish was over I checked my shoulder. I was okay. I found out later that my brother was wounded, taking a piece of shrapnel in his left shoulder."

Finishing his debriefing, Louis said, "We rescued our patrol. Called in an air strike, then lit up Pusan like the Fourth of July. Mission accomplished."

Louis hurried over to the base hospital to check on Frank. "What happened, Frank?" he asked. "When did you get hit?"

"I was leading the attack," Frank explained, "when a grenade blast knocked me to the ground. I remember calling to the medic, then I passed out."

Louis noted, "I can't believe it. When you went down I felt the pain of your wound. It was like I was hit. It was an eerie feeling."

Frank said, "It probably was just a coincidence. Let's check it out with the shrink."

"No way," Louis declared, "we don't want to end up in the psycho ward. They will think we're crazy."

Chapter 9
Election/Battle/Serious Concern

November 1949, election day. Snow fell all during the night, leaving a heavy blanket of white covering Drew. Polling places had to be dug out from under two-foot drifts to make way for the citizens to cast their ballots in what would be a tight mayoral race. Betty and Katrina arrived in town early, attended Mass and received Father Lazlo's blessing.

The morning vote was slow coming in. Weather conditions had worsened, which seemed to set a trend favoring the incumbent mayor. Louis declared, "We have to get out the vote. Call a meeting of our party workers, put shovels in their hands and get our people to the polls."

By midday, Louis's plan was beginning to slowly turn the tide. Later that day, as the polls closed, it was too close to call. At his campaign headquarters, Louis, his family and his volunteers watched anxiously as the numbers started to roll in. It was a seesaw race. At midnight all but two precincts had tallied their votes. There were a possible twenty votes left if everyone had cast a ballot. These were rural polling sites and anything could happen. As it now stood, the incumbent mayor led by a mere three votes. At 12:20 am a pollster arrived with the final tally.

Louis felt a surge of adrenaline. Those were farmers from immigrant families like himself. Would they believe in him? Twelve of possible 20 votes were cast. All in favor of the new mayor-elect, Louis Varga. They celebrated into the early hours of the morning, and then Louis thanked everyone and went home with his family.

May 1950. The war in Korea raged on. Peace talks at Pamyunjong established a line of demarcation at the 38th parallel, splitting the country in half. A cease-fire was declared, but the warring factions could not decide on the simplest of rules to set down and talk. Months went by and the talks continued, only to fail session after session. Atrocities committed in the guise of war were mounting up against the North. Infuriated, the Allied Forces, backed by the Geneva Convention, promised retaliation by forming a wartime tribunal to capture and convict those charged with war crimes.

In Osaka, Louis and Frank were weary of the many assaults they and their crews were making. They hoped for a respite to celebrate their birthdays. After a month's rest, Frank's wound had healed and he was back in action. Junior led his men into enemy territory on a dozen occasions during Frank's absence. The fighting was fierce and deadly. The jungle was thick with enemy troops. Snipers firing from trees killed and wounded his men all around him, but slowly they were sought out and left dangling in the tree branches, dead.

On May 29, the day before the twins twenty-fourth birthday, the call to duty came again. This was to be an all-out offensive to gain control of a strategic mountaintop that had been held by both sides. It controlled the valley below, and in the hands of the enemy gave them a virtual stronghold, preventing any advance to the port city of Pusan, the allies' main objective. Every available helicopter was rolled out on the tarmac, and flight crews worked feverishly arming and fueling the birds. Pilots went through their pre-flight checklist as the assault team, ready for action, boarded for takeoff. At six am the birds began to leave the nest. Twenty-five copters fluttered skyward, their whirling blades kicking up clouds of dust as each Huey lifted off. Rising up into V-shaped formations, like flocks of geese they noisily winged their way toward a destiny yet unknown.

The Varga lieutenants gave thumbs-up signs as they parted company on their way into battle. Apprehension welled up in their minds as they neared the jump-off site, but quickly turned to the job at hand. Rockets and small arms fire greeted the squadron as they begin to settle onto the valley floor. Two birds exploded in mid-air and crashed in flaming fireballs. Junior's squad gathered on the ground. Shouting orders, he moved his men forward, joining up with other crews safely positioned at the base of the mountain. Braving artillery, mortar and machine gun fire, the men began inching their way up the incline. The gun ships, under a continuous barrage of rocket fire, laid down smoke for cover. The next wave followed, dropping ravaging napalm across the mountaintop and scorching everything in sight. Halfway up the steep hill the enemy fire was so intense that orders came down to dig in and regroup.

Colonel Barret, commanding the operation, called his junior officers together to implement a new strategy. He spoke calmly but with authority

"We are suffering too many casualties on this damn mountain trying to crawl our way up. Squad leaders, order your men to retreat to the valley floor." The colonel continued, "The gun ships will cease all activity and return to the drop site. Get all the men back into the copters; we're going in low and drop in on those SOBs. Lieutenant Varga, you and your brother's squad will make an observation flyover at the top. Get me numbers and locations of men and equipment. Pinpoint artillery and high volume of ground troops, and then get back here fast. We need that input. Go, and good hunting."

Over the mountaintops the Hueys were tossed about from near hits by enemy fire. After the initial flyover, Louis was not convinced he had all the data he needed. He ordered the pilot to make a return pass. The pilot objected, saying, "Lieutenant, that flack is murder. You're pushing your luck."

"Do it," Louis ordered.

The next few minutes were chaotic.

"Were hit!" the pilot cried. "I'm losing control! We're going down!"

Then silence.

Frank watched in horror as his brother's bird spun, crashing into the mountainside. He radioed back, "Copter One down, returning to base."

Lieutenant Frank Varga awoke and looked around through half-closed eyes, wondering where he was and why his body felt bruised and beaten. He tried to get up but fell back, pain coursing through his body from head to toe. He lay there calling out for help, trying to grasp reality, but to no avail. The noise in his head was deafening, the pain excruciating. Then there was nothing.

Louis Varga Junior, Lieutenant, U.S. Army, lay close to death in a hospital room in Osaka, Japan, after being rescued when the chopper he was in was shot out of the sky and crashed. His battered and bloodied body pulsated as doctors worked frantically to stabilize his critical condition. In the next room, his brother Frank was suffering the same trauma, but unlike Louis he had no visible wounds.

"He is in shock," the doctor pronounced. "Medicate him and we'll check on him in 24 hours." The next day Frank's condition had not gotten any better, so a psychiatrist was called in to evaluate his puzzling condition.

Chapter 10
Psychosomatic/Home/Wedding

A telegram arrived at the Varga's home. Katrina, home alone, answered the door. With trembling hands, she accepted the wire from the Department of the Army. She could not get herself to open it, fearful that the message contained terrible news about her grandsons. She called the mayor's office and spoke to Louis, who then contacted Betty and the girls. At home, Louis opened the telegram and silently read the bold words that jumped out at him. Then he spoke aloud, "The boys are alive. Junior has been seriously wounded and Frank is in shock. Further information will follow."

A week had passed since the critical battle at the mountaintop. The enemy had resisted fiercely but was beaten back. The combatants paid a terrible price in the death toll and wounded. Louis had regained consciousness, but was still in critical condition. The doctor treating Frank determined his condition as psychosomatic. In twin births, the bond between siblings can be so strong that on many occasions one's mind or physical affliction is transferred to the other, and they suffer through it together.

The war was over for the Varga twins. In late August Louis was discharged from the hospital, his wounds sufficiently healed, but months of physical therapy lay ahead.

Frank's condition eased as his brother convalesced. The psychosomatic experience the boys had been through was explained in detail, so if any further incidents occurred they would know how to deal wth them. Louis was transferred to the Tripler Army and Navy Hospital, on the island of Oahu in Hawaii, for three months of intense therapy. Frank was assigned duty at Hickem Field, not far from the hospital.

When the news of the twin's transfer arrived at home, Louis and Betty decided that a trip to Hawaii to visit their sons would be the best thing they could do for themselves and the boys. At 78, and not in the best of health, Katrina opted to stay home with Violet and Grace, who would have loved to go but were needed at their jobs. All they asked was that the boys call them. On Christmas Eve, Louis and Betty deplaned at the Honolulu International Airport, eager to see their sons. Their first get-together in six months was a tearful and joyous reunion. They talked for hours. The boys relieved their terrible experiences in Korea and were thankful they survived. Louis and Betty talked about home, Katrina and the girls. Later that evening, Junior and Frank spoke with their sweethearts and grandmother.

Christmas Day was a special day. At a brief military awards ceremony, Lieutenants Louis and Frank Varga were decorated with Purple Hearts for wounds received in battle, and promoted to captains effective on January 1, 1951. They were re-assigned to their former duty station in Osaka, Japan, for one year as training officers.

Back home in Drew, all was not well. Katrina, tired and in failing health, was often bedridden. Betty relinquished all her outside duties to stay home and care for her and the household. When Violet and Grace where home they were a positive force, and assisted Betty in every way they could.

Beginning his first year as mayor, Louis wanted to thank his Hungarian constituents for their help in getting him elected. He formed the Hungarian Relief Society, or HRS. With the help of the banking community and some of the more affluent families in Drew, the society offered financial aid to those families wanting to borrow money for care packages, or to sponsor and pay for an immigrant's passage to the new world.

December 1950. Louis and Frank were coming home. Their tour of duty in Japan concluded, they were reassigned to Fort Sill, Oklahoma, as battalion officers. Before taking over their new command they were granted a well-earned leave of absence. The long flight home seemed endless, but three days before Christmas they were in the arms of their loved ones. Reunited with their fiancees, for the first time since they left for Japan the boys wined and dined the girls, getting to know them all over again. Their love for each other had not waned. The old cliché, "absence makes the heart grow fonder," proved to be a truism. Talk of marriage and wedding preparations were of prime interest, with the wedding ceremony the most important topic. A June wedding was preferable.

However, Katrina's illness could necessitate an earlier date. She was slowly slipping away, and the doctor held out little hope she would last until June. A wedding without their beloved grandmother was out of the question. They would get married February 14, Valentine's Day.

Reporting for duty at Fort Sill, the captains went through orientation and were assigned their first platoon of recruits. They were assisted by drill sergeants who were veterans of World War II and hardened combat soldiers who had fought in the Pacific against the Japanese. They made Louis and Frank's job easy.

Church bells sounded their joyful invitation to gather together and celebrate a holy and happy event. Our Lady of Hungary Church was filled to capacity to witness the double marriage ceremony of Captains Louis Varga Junior and Frank Varga to Violet Spencer and Grace Hunter. The tiny church was filled with flowers and decorated in red and white valentine hearts, signs of love and purity. At the altar, the grooms and their best men, dressed in full military uniform, stood at attention, awaiting their brides-to-be.

The doors at the front of the church opened, and the procession begin moving down the white carpeted aisle. A flower girl dropped red and white rose petals in the path of the brides as they commenced their walk to the altar.

Violet, dressed in a shimmering white gown with a long train, stepped lightly as she moved to meet her fiance. Her long dark hair curled down her back, and against the white of the dress it shown like a sunrise. Her veiled continence could not hide her beauty and the loving smile that parted her lips. Grace followed a few steps behind. Her tall, full figured body eased gracefully down the aisle, dressed in a wedding gown alike in all respects to Violet's. Her black hair and brown eyes were like a silhouette against her gleaming white dress. Her effervescent smile glowed, lighting up her young face. Father Lazlo greeted the girls with a smile and motioned the twins to step to the altar. The church grew silent as the old priest began the wedding ceremony. The vows were spoken, the rings exchanged, and as they knelt before the priest and their God, he pronounced them husband and wife. Applause broke the silence as the couples embraced and kissed, acknowledging their love for each other. Turning, they exited the church with the cheers and good wishes of family and friends.

A celebration such as was never seen in Drew greeted the newlyweds that evening. Food and drink, music and dancing, speeches and toasts filled the town hall with gaiety and laughter. The next morning the two couples departed on a brief honeymoon, then on to Fort Sill and new homes outside the base compound.

Louis and Betty sat having breakfast the morning after the wedding reliving the beautiful events of Valentine's Day. With them were Violet's parents, who had just returned from a European vacation, and Grace's mother and oldest brother. The Spencers were well-to-do, gracious people, but enjoyed the company of the jet-set, traveling around the world from party to party. They loved their daughter, but after they put her through school they left her on her own, with a sizable sum of money to fend for herself. Mrs. Hunter and her son, Timothy, apart from the rest of the family, were truly loving and wonderful people. The difficulties that confronted the family were painful, and the breakup left mental scars, especially on Mother Hunter.

Chapter 11
Katrina

Under close scrutiny by her doctor, Katrina Varga was in a wheelchair and was able to watch and enjoy the wedding of her grandsons. It was one of the most festive days of her life. She though of her dear husband, Julius, and longtime friends, Frank and Gizella, and how proud they would have been. She thanked God for the strength he gave her to witness what she knew might be her last triumph on earth

May 1951. The fighting in Korea escalated. Peace talks broke down time after time. America's young people were becoming defiant. Riots by college students broke out, only to be quelled by police and National Guard troops using tear gas and batons. Draft-age men burned their draft cards and fled over the border into Canada. The country was in an upheaval. Discontent was the order of the day.

At Fort Sill, the platoon of recruits training under the leadership of Captains Louis and Frank Varga had just finished weeks of intensive simulated jungle warfare. During the graduation ceremony, a telegram from Drew stirred an emotional fever in the heart of Violet. She immediately called Grace and sent an orderly with a message to Louis on the parade grounds. Frank took the message, and he and Louis excused themselves and left the reviewing stands. The message read that Grandmother Varga was in the hospital, near death. They were asked to please come home as soon as possible. The next morning the boys requested and were granted an emergency furlough.

At the hospital, Betty, Louis and Father Lazlo gathered in Katrina's room, watching helplessly as she lay in her bed, laboring desperately with every breath. The doctors said they could do nothing more except to make her as comfortable as possible. Louis and Betty prayed with the good Father as he anointed Katrina in the last rites of the church. A few hours later Louis Junior, Frank and the girls arrived in Drew and went directly to the hospital. Katrina opened her eyes momentarily. Looking around through blurred vision, she was able to make out members of her family and Father Lazlo. She spoke so softly to the old priest that he had to put his ear close to her mouth to hear her. After a few moments he nodded and took his rosary from his pocket and began reciting the Glorious Mysteries with her in Hungarian. Although she could barely speak, her lips moved as she responded to the prayers. Halfway through the beads, her body went limp and her soul rose peacefully into the arms of her Savior. Katrina Varga was 79 years old.

The solemn funeral procession wove its way through the streets of Drew, stopping at the Church of Our Lady. Inside, Father Lazlo awaited the remains of Katrina Varga. Six of her countrymen carried her casket, draped in both an American and Hungarian Flag. Now as it sat at the foot of the altar, Father Lazlo covered it with the white cloth that symbolized her baptism into the church and to the Father, Son and Holy Ghost. The Mass of Christian Burial was intoned by the priest and Our Lady's choir. After the final blessing, the procession resumed to the Varga home and her final resting place. She was laid to her eternal rest next to Julius, her loving husband, her granddaughter and lifelong friend, Gizella Horvath.

After a brief period of mourning, the Varga twins and their wives returned to Fort Sill. Betty and Louis, deep in their grief, sadly waved farewell and returned to their now empty house. Pictures and personal items throughout the house would serve as reminders of their parents, and their memories would be kept alive in their hearts.

Chapter 12
A Journey/Rescue/Wounded

The Hungarian Relief Society was hard at work trying to keep up with the many applications from families requesting immigration to the shores of America. The committee screening the applicants were thorough and fair in their assessment, and only after careful consideration were the applications approved and sent to Louis, who had been named director, for a final decision. By the end of 1951, ten new families were added to the increasing population of Drew, and the society's work was applauded by its citizens.

During Christmas week, Louis and Betty visited their children at Fort Sill. Betty and the girls went shopping while Louis was given the grand tour of the base. On Christmas Eve they all went to midnight Mass at the base chapel. On Christmas Day, at dinner, Louis surprised the family when he said, "Your mother and I are going to Hungary. We have given it a lot of thought, and we want to visit our parents' homeland to see for ourselves all the things they talked about."

Junior cut off his father. "You know that the Hungarian government is under the rule of the Communists, with a dictator as their leader."

"Yes, I am aware of that," Louis responded, "but the American Consulate said it is safe to travel there provided we follow the rules."

June 1952. The war room at the White House was in extraordinary session. Intelligence agents were reporting the capture of an American general by North Korean forces. ROK commandos abducted the general, an observer and forward command strategist, from his quarters. His knowledge of military secrets made it imperative that his rescue be accomplished ASAP. It would be a serious breech of national security if he were to give up any information. All high-level Army commanders were to appoint or request volunteers for this highly dangerous mission. At the Pentagon, the names of military personnel qualified to engage in the rescue attempt were being scrutinized. Eight men, including two officers, one master sergeant and five enlisted men, were to be selected. After screening the names of the applicants, the names of three squads were delivered to the White House for final selection. In the situation room the decision was made, and the individuals were notified. Fort Sill was designated as the home base, where final preparations would be completed.

Captains Louis and Frank Varga, much to the chagrin of their wives, volunteered for the perilous mission. When the word came down, only Frank was chosen. Junior's physical condition and the trauma he went through persuaded the Army that he was unfit for duty; however, he would assist in the training and briefing.

Before their parents left for Hungary, the twins, Violet and Grace made a surprise weekend visit to tell them they were going to be parents. All of them were ecstatic with their good fortune, that both girls had conceived around the same time.

When they arrived and told them the news, Louis said, "This calls for a celebration. Champagne to toast you all and our future grandchildren."

The following morning, after saying goodbye to the children, Betty and Louis left Lincoln International Airport on their odyssey to the land of their parents. In Hungary, the Vargas were enjoying their sightseeing. Restrictions in some areas curtailed their movements, but the hindrance did not quell their interest or overcome their desire to journey into the paths of their forefathers. While stopping in Budapest, news out of Korea caught their attention. A small group of U.S. Army commandos had successfully infiltrated a POW camp and rescued a high-ranking American general. Two Americans were killed and one seriously wounded in the daring daylight raid. The names of the deceased and wounded were being withheld until notification of next of kin. Unaware that Frank was involved in the raid, they continued on their tour without further information.

In Japan, the bodies of the two American soldiers killed during the raid rescuing the American general were placed aboard a C-17 transport plane, in flag-draped coffins, on their way home to their final resting place at Arlington National Cemetery. Upon arrival at Landover Air Force Base, they were met by six uniformed pallbearers, placed on a horse-bearing caisson and escorted in highest military tradition to their place of interment. A 21-gun salute echoed throughout the rows of white crosses, and as a final tribute to the fallen heroes, a bugler blew the melancholy notes of taps, signifying a final goodbye.

Louis Varga Junior paced nervously as the hour his brother's mission was taking place in Korea. Sweat trickled down his face as in his mind he led the assault on the POW camp. In a trance, he traced the steps of the squad as they searched their way into the enemy compound, opening and closing doors, seeking their prize. Suddenly, gunfire broke the silence of the early morning assault. They had been discovered and all hell broke loose. Then, as quick as it began, it was over. Louis recoiled and went twisting to the floor. His mind snapped back to reality.

"My God," he said, "Frank's been hit. I know what's happening, I can't panic. Violet, help me." Then he passed out.

Louis and Betty were about to board their plane for the trip back home when the airport PA system blared out, "Louis Varga, report to the information desk." Surprised but unconcerned, he and Betty found their way to the information desk and were greeted by a messenger from the American Consulate. Driving to the embassy, Louis questioned the messenger as to why they were being delayed, but he said he was not aware of what was going on. The ambassador welcomed them, then reported that their son, Captain Frank Varga, had been seriously wounded in a rescue mission in Korea.

Louis questioned the truth of his information. "My sons have been classified noncombatants," he declared. "How could this be?"

The ambassador replied, "I'm sure the Army will be able to fill you in on the details. I am sorry I cannot help you."

Back at the airport, the couple boarded their plane, agonizing over the events of the past as they winged their way home.

In Japan, Captain Frank Varga convalesced in the intensive care unit from surgery, necessitated by wounds received in battle. He was in jeopardy of losing his right leg, which was mangled by a grenade blast. Strengthened by the love for his wife and unborn child, he fought desperately to overcome adversity and return home a whole person.

Violet heard Louis cry out. Rushing to the bedroom, she found him lying on the floor, rolling around, grasping his right leg and screaming in pain. Having been made aware of his physiological condition, she was able to calm him down sufficiently and help him into bed. She realized Frank must be in grave danger if his anxiety and pain was being manifested in Louis. She knew that as Frank grew better or worse, so would Louis.

Chapter 13
Louis Senior/Babies

July 4, 1952. The Varga clan gathered together to celebrate the birth of the American nation. Betty and Louis regaled the children with wonderful stories of their trip to Hungary and how much they enjoyed seeing their ancestral homeland. After the nostalgic interlude, Frank painfully got out of his chair and walked around the room with a perceptible limp, which he would have the rest of his life.

Junior jokingly told his brother, "Cease and desist getting injured. I can't handle it," and everyone had a lighthearted chuckle. At 50 years old, Betty and Louis were in the prime of their life. Their business empire had grown, and financially they were well-to-do. Their boys, now 26, married and expecting their first babies, were in their third year of military service and debating whether to stay in the Army or venture into civilian life. At the urging of their wives, who had experienced the horrors of war through their husband's eyes, they considered leaving the military. Their problem seemed to be solved when orders from the Pentagon relieved them of duty at Fort Sill and ordered them to report to the commandant at West Point. Surprised, to say the least, the boys debated as to what the Army had in store for them.

***

Sitting in the mayor's office, Louis felt a wave of nausea sweep over him. He began sweating profusely as the pain in his chest doubled him over. Calling to his secretary, he got up and stumbled to the door. At the hospital, Betty leaned over and kissed his cheek. Miss Taylor, her friend and husband's secretary, indicated that Louis most likely suffered a heart attack. The doctor in the emergency room corroborated her tentative diagnosis that it indeed was a heart attack. After further examinations and tests it was found that there was slight damage to the heart, and clogged arteries would have to be cleaned out. That evening Louis underwent surgery to eliminate the blockages.

Alarmed by Louis's condition, the family talked over the situation. Betty would stay at her husband's side. The deputy mayor would run the city's business until Louis returned to the office. The boys had no choice; they had to report as ordered. Violet and Grace, not sure what the Army had in store for their husbands, would remain at home until that issue was settled.

In August, Frank and Louis reported as ordered to the commandant at West Point. After a long meeting, they emerged from his office, beaming with pride. They called home immediately and broke the news to the family. They had been offered and accepted positions as instructors on the staff of West Point, effective September 1, 1953. Until then they had been assigned duty as recruiting officers in Lincoln.

Christmas 1952. Joy to the world seemed most appropriate for the Varga family. Louis was well on his way to a full recovery. The boys commuted daily and spent weekends at home with their wives. Betty pampered Violet and Grace, watching over them like a mother hen. With their careers seemingly set in stone, moving to upstate New York was a necessity. Finding suitable homes was a priority. Early in January, with their exceedingly pregnant spouses in tow, Louis, Frank and the girls boarded a plane to New York.

On the return trip, buoyed by their success in finding a beautiful duplex house, the foursome were excitedly chatting and planning how each would furnish their new homes. Suddenly, the pilot interrupted their conversation with an announcement over the intercom that they may experience turbulence over the Great Lakes, and to fasten their seat belts. As they neared Lake Michigan, the plane began to vibrate and toss around. Unaccustomed to flying in their delicate conditions, the girls became frightened. The plane dropped several hundred feet, shaking up the passengers and creating a moment of panic. Junior and Frank tried to reassure the girls that everything would be all right, but nothing they said could comfort them. Both ladies were becoming stressful. Air sick and nauseated, they began to complain of stomach pains. Junior called the flight attendant to see if she could help, but she felt the girls needed a doctor. Setting a few rows behind them, an elderly woman rose from her seat and moved forward.

"Can I be of help?" she asked. "I am a nurse."

She did an examination, asked questions and stated calmly that they were both going to be fine. Speaking to the attendant, she said, "Tell the pilot to radio ahead and have an ambulance standing by, ready to take the girls directly to the hospital."

Louis then made a call to Drew to advise his parents as to what was happening. When the plane arrived in Lincoln, the girls were rushed to the hospital. Doctors quickly examined them, gave them a mild sedative and told them they and the babies were fine.

Louis, with renewed vigor, threw himself into his role as mayor. During his period of convalescence he had given a lot of thought to expanding his role in government politics. As a prominent figure in Nebraska politics he had many friends and staunch advocates that could boost his candidacy for a state or even national office. With the next election two years away, he had ample time to campaign, provided he could get the backing of his party bigwigs.

March 1953. Easter Sunday morning. The Varga family attended the sunrise Mass at Our Lady's Church. After breakfast, Violet and Grace were tired from their early awakening and both settled down for a nap. A couple hours later, Violet awoke, called Junior and said, "I am having contractions. It's time to go to the hospital." Grace complained of back pain and anticipated her time was also near. They were both bundled up and taken to the hospital.

It was March 24, the holiest and most joyous day of the year in the Catholic Church. It was this day that the Vargas celebrated the birth of their children and grandchildren. Louis and Betty waited anxiously, praying that the mothers and babies come through childbirth without complications. Their minds reflected back 26 years earlier to the day their sons were born. Meanwhile, Junior and Frank nervously paced the waiting room floor.

What seemed like hours were just minutes. The doctors burst into the waiting room and announced, "Boys, you each have a beautiful, healthy daughter."

In their bed rooms, Violet and Grace were tired but happy, and cuddled their newborn daughters. Hugs, kisses and words of praise for their brave wives dominated the jubilant scene as the fathers strutted about, congratulating each other and claiming that the babies looked like them. Quite to the contrary, the babies were visions of their mothers, beautiful and gratefully so. Louis and Betty were all smiles as they took turns holding the precious bundles of joy, calling each other grandma and grandpa. On the way home, Betty and Louis talked about their parents and how proud they would have been had they lived to see their great-grandchildren.

Chapter 14
Baby's Names/Father Lazlo/ Louis

Two weeks after the Varga babies were born, they went to Our Lady's Church for the first time to be baptized. There had been no mention of names for the children. When asked, the parents said wait and see. Close friends were chosen as godparents, and Father Lazlo would perform the ceremony.

Louis Junior and Violet watched the good priest pour the holy water over their child's head while proclaiming, "Katrina Julienne Varga, I baptize you in the name of the Father, Son and Holy Ghost. Amen."

Then Grace and Frank stepped forward and listened to their child's godparents speak the baptismal vows as Father Lazlo christened Francine Gizella Varga.

Betty and Louis were overwhelmed with their choices of names for their granddaughters. Junior spoke up, saying, "We loved our grandparents and want to keep them in our hearts by giving our children their names. Violet and Grace said it would be an honor and consented, and we knew it would please you. Now the fourth generation of Horvaths and Vargas will carry on in memory of the first."

***

The message was splashed over newspaper headlines. TV and radio broadcasts throughout the world echoed the news that the hot war in Korea was over, replaced by a politically motivated cold war behind the bamboo curtain of the communist Republic of Korea. Thousands of GIs gave up their lives in a country torn by civil strife. Drawn into the war first as advisors, the noose tightened around America's neck, and before we knew it we had a fight on our hands. It was an unpopular war, with much of the nation against it, especially our young fighting men who fought and died for their country but were unappreciated and humiliated by those they fought for.

Postwar America slipped into a recession. Veterans that came home looking for their old jobs were turned away and told there were no openings available. Jobless and homeless, the scourge of alcohol and drugs became a way of life for the most despondent. In Drew, the situation was most prevalent among American-Hungarian youth, but the city fathers, and especially Mayor Varga, would not let these young men be ostracized and fall victim to a life of drug and alcohol addiction. The Hungarian Relief Society stepped in, providing menial labor and loans with minimal interest payments to those who were willing to work and contribute to the welfare of the city. This action by Louis as mayor was another credit and accomplishment that would enhance his resume for seeking office in the upcoming election.

August 1953. Their recruiting days over, the Varga twins and their precious families were preparing to leave the homestead and head for West Point.

"Promise you will visit us?" asked Violet.

"We will," Betty acknowledged.

Junior asked, "Why don't you sell out and move to New York?"

"No way, son," his father replied. "I have unfinished business to take care of. Perhaps sometime in the future." Indeed, Louis had plans, but for now they were just tentative.

Father Lazlo, the beloved priest of Our Lady, was getting old. He worried that he would no longer be able to carry out the functions of his priesthood. His health was failing, and he yearned to return to Hungary before he died. The Bishop in Lincoln had no other Hungarian priest to take over his duties, and the good Father did not want to leave his parish without a Hungarian-speaking successor. Louis was aware of Father Lazlo's dilemma, and when he came to him with a request, Louis promised to help him. Through the Hungarian Relief Society, a request was forwarded to the Holy See in Rome, asking the Pope to allow Father Lazlo to return to his homeland and replace him with a native-born Hungarian prelate.

Weeks went by, but finally on Thanksgiving Day, a telegram arrived from Cardinal Ferency, apostolic head of the Catholic Church in Hungary. He apologized for the long delay in answering, stating that the Communist-run state was harassing the Catholic Church and refusing to allow his priests passports to leave the country.

"I have the ideal young priest who wants to come to America and is willing to take the chance, but it would be a dangerous journey. With your organization's contacts and financial aid, we will send him on his way as soon as we hear from you." It was signed, "your servant, Cardinal Joseph Ferency."

The party faithful from Drew and up through the nation's capitol had been in high-level meetings, compiling facts and figures to determine the elective status of Louis Varga. The Nebraska governor's race was wide open, as well as a seat in the third district of the House of Representatives of the U.S. Congress. Both could be ably filled by the popular mayor of Drew. It was left up to him to decide which office to run for.

In mid-December an old-fashioned winter storm hit the plains states, then roared through the Midwest and didn't stop until it reached the eastern seaboard. Snow and ice covered the country, leaving in its wake downed trees and power lines. Electrical outages put life at risk for thousands. Food and water shortages added to the misery. Transportation came to a standstill. The hardest hit was the airline industry. Hundreds of flights were canceled, and with the Christmas season not far off, thousands of passengers could be stranded over the holidays. The airlines stood to lose millions in revenue, but in the long run the flying public would pay with escalated ticket prices. A phone call from Betty to her children left them disappointed. A Christmas visit to West Point was out of the question; however, they would fly in for the birthdays of their grandchildren.

Word arrived from Cardinal Ferency in Hungary that Drew's new priest was on his way. He was welcomed by Father Lazlo. Moreover, the young man, at his request, was being accompanied by his parents.

Christmas Eve. Father Lazlo and Father Herzog celebrated midnight Mass. The youthful priest gave his first sermon, and his enthusiasm and way with words put Father Lazlo at ease.

Father Lazlo knew that the young man would shepherd his flock well.

January 1954. Louis was on the campaign trail. He had opted to try and unseat the veteran congressman from the third congressional district of Nebraska. His precinct, one of several hundred, was a solid block and could be counted on to carry him to victory, but the rest he had to stump and try and win over the incumbent's followers.

Betty was in a happy mood and was packing suitcases for their visit to see their children and grandchildren. Louis arrived home after seeing Father Lazlo off on his trip back to his homeland. A phone call interrupted his conversation with Betty, and the call left a puzzled look on his face.

Betty asked, "What's wrong, dear?"

Louis answered, "They want me to campaign the week of our vacation. They say it's very important because Jesse, the man I'm running against, will be in the area, and they want me to debate him. I have to go. I hope the kids understand."

It was a gala birthday party for one-year-old Katrina and Gizella. Neighborhood toddlers and their mothers shared in the festivities of the day with Violet, Grace and Betty. Junior and Frank took time out from their duties to help their daughters blow out their big candle. After the party, the children were tucked in bed and the adults sat down and talked. They were all disappointed that Louis was not here with them, but Betty explained the situation and how badly he felt missing the girls' first birthday, and that he would make it up to all of them.

***

Louis Varga was tired, but he would not admit it to anyone. Constantly on the go, making speeches, not eating properly or sleeping regularly was beginning to take a toll on him. Betty could see a change coming over him but kept silent. He will tell me if anything is wrong, she thought.

Driving back to Drew late one night after a long day of speeches, handshakes and fast food, Louis felt sick to his stomach. Thinking he had indigestion, he stopped at a service station and purchased antacid medication. He felt some relief as he continued homeward. An hour from home he was jolted with a severe pain in his chest. Instinctively, he pulled the car off the highway. Gasping for breath, he thought, My God, I'm going to die. As he sat there, he realized how selfish he was, thinking of his own interests and political aspirations, and how he had taken time away from his loved ones. Tired and in pain, he dozed off. When he awoke it was daylight. He roused himself and started for home. All the way there he sought answers to the questions running through his mind. Finally, he pulled into his driveway and was greeted by his very worried wife

"Where have you been?" Betty asked. "I called and they said you left last evening. I have been out of my mind wondering if something had happened to you."

"Something did happen," Louis replied, "I think I had another heart attack."

After a brief rest period, Betty took Louis to the hospital for a checkup. Doctors monitored his heart while they put him through a stress test, ran a battery of blood tests and finally a cardiograph. An hour later he was told he had suffered a mild heart attack, but damage to the heart was negligible.

The doctor told Louis, "You should be in better health at your age. You have to change your lifestyle. Slow down, take a vacation, enjoy life and ease up on your work schedule."

Spring passed without incident. Louis stayed close to home,

avoiding any strenuous work while he pondered one of the toughest decisions of his life

On July 4, a barbecue at the Varga farm hosted delegates from all over the third district. They were there to champion their candidate into the stretch run in the November elections. Good food, friendly camaraderie and copious amounts of beer, wine and bourbon got the crowd into a wildly cheering, name-calling frenzy.

"We want Louis, we want Louis," chanted the crowd. After fifteen minutes he gave in and mounted the soap box, smiling and waving to quiet the mass of humanity. His first few words drew comments from the crowd. Louis stood his ground and repeated his statement.

"I have decided I will not be a candidate for congress. I am sorry I waited so long in telling you, but my health and devotion to my family is my primary concern. I thank all of you who have worked so hard for my election, and hope you will understand my motives are truthful and sincere."

Chapter 15
Farewell

As a lame duck mayor, Louis turned over his duties to his deputy mayor, cleaned out his office and bid farewell to his staff. He stopped to visit Father Herzog and his parents. They were living together in the only room in the small church, but they were forever grateful for the kindness Louis had shown by bringing then here. Father Lazlo, back in Hungary, addressed the concerns of his people by requesting the relief society to bring more desperate families to America. Touched by the sincerity of the old priest, Louis considered doing more for his Hungarian brethren, both in America and in the old country. With Betty in full accord with his plan, Louis set about selling all his physical property, except the living quarters on the farm. He closed out his stock portfolio, selling everything he had. He claimed a huge profit and put much of it in a trust fund for his granddaughters.

January 1, 1955. He quietly hired a local construction firm to build a new rectory for Our Lady's Church in honor of Father Lazlo. In March, Louis and Betty flew to New York, where they filed a will with an attorney, consulted a banking firm and deposited their life savings. Then it was on to West Point and a family gathering

March 24. The Varga daughters were two years old. Louis was amazed at how the girls had grown, and how cute and cuddly they were. He saw in each of them their namesakes, and spoke their names with pride and love. After dinner, when the children were put to bed, Louis and Betty told their children the events of the past year and his plans for the future, including moving to Long Island permanently. The family was jubilant with the news and asked how soon.

"It won't be to long," Louis said. "I have some unfinished business to take care of. When that is over and done, we will be back to stay."

It was a lovely summer day when Louis and Betty flew out of Lincoln on a final trip to Hungary. Landing in Budapest, they traveled by train and bus to the village their parents once lived in. Making inquires of families with the names Horvath and Varga, they found several and contacted each of them. Luckily, two young brothers, Steven and Charles Varga, and two young ladies, Irma and Theresa Horvath, were living nearby. All four were neighbors, single and lived with their parents on the family farms. Asked if they would like to immigrate to America, the young people jumped at the opportunity. Their mothers and fathers were not really happy with the idea, and declined, but if the children wished to go they would give them their blessing and perhaps someday change their minds and come to live with them in America. It was not hard to see that the boys and girls were interested in each other, which made for the ideal situation.

It was like 1903 all over again. The Horvaths and Vargas traveled from the old country to Drew, Nebraska. This time without the hardships and worries that confronted the first immigrants. There were two charming homes waiting for them, in lieu of cabins. There was a grown-up city nearby with a population of three generations of Hungarian-Americans. There was a church, school and, best of all, the opportunity to grow and prosper in a land where all people can be free of tyranny and oppression; a land where dreams can come true for all people who love the American way of life. So it was for the new immigrants.

In a final farewell, they visited their longtime friends in Drew, thanking them and their parents and wishing them good health and all the happiness the good Lord would allow. There was one last prayerful stop at Our Lady's Church, with a blessing from Father Herzog, then a tearful goodbye at the family burial plot.

At the West Point homes of their children, the telephones rang. Louis Junior picked up the phone, listened for a moment and hung up. Then he jubilantly announced, "Mom and Dad are on their way."

Printed in the United States
41798LVS00006B/44